Searching

for the

City of

Love

A N N A   Q U I M P O   M A G U I R E

authorHOUSE®

AuthorHouse™
1663 Liberty Drive
Bloomington, IN 47403
www.authorhouse.com
Phone: 1 (800) 839-8640

Published by AuthorHouse   11/08/2016

ISBN: 978-1-5246-4937-1 (sc)
ISBN: 978-1-5246-4935-7 (hc)
ISBN: 978-1-5246-4936-4 (e)

Library of Congress Control Number: 2016918656

Print information available on the last page.

Any people depicted in stock imagery provided by Thinkstock are models, and such images are being used for illustrative purposes only. Certain stock imagery © *Thinkstock.*

This book is printed on acid-free paper.

Contents

The city of love does not exist

Beauty runs through every city

It would be hard to choose between pine trees and skyscrapers

And I can't decide whether roaming around busy streets would beat hiking through a meadow

There are lovely cities unrecognized

To fall in love with too

Wanderer

I am not a sight to see

I am not the Eiffel Tower

I will not take your breath away
like the Sagrada Família

And I'm not as calm as the Swiss Alp breeze

But fall in love with the cities I've seen

And scatter my heart along their streets

I'm always broken when I leave

Please Don't Let Me Go Back

I can't count on both hands what I've learned from this life that's as fast paced as an interstate freeway but a couple of things come to mind

I don't know if all this wandering has made me realize that home is not a place, rather a state of mind.

I think we are all on a journey without a destination.

I'm not sure if we have a complete path laid out in front of us.

I've felt like I've been through all the twists and turns, left and right, up and down. Will I continue to travel down this path or take a detour back to my old ways?

Grey

I want to be under the English sky

To soak in the tears from the clouds above

Let the mysterious grey cast down on me

Count on Me

And I've crossed the ocean, my dear.

I've climbed up taller mountains

Swam through water clearer than your blue eyes

I've watched many sunsets without you,

Because the endings aren't so bad anymore

I realize now that I can't spend the rest of my life coming back to you

Because I've seen new people

Whether it'd be the hundred that have passed by my table outside the café

Or the one that sat across from me on the two hour train ride

I've fallen in love with being alone.

It's taken me for what seems an eternity because I've been right here all along.

The Only Fear When Leaving

*It's taking every ounce of self-control in my
body not to run up to you and leap into your
arms to hold your face and kiss your lips.*

*I can't count how many times I've taken a
breath and held my tongue because I didn't
want to reveal any words that would cause
us to continue to desire each other.*

*All of me wants to tell you how I feel. Every bone,
every strand of hair, every particle, every cell in
my body knows we can become something more.*

I know I'm going to fall in love with you.

And I want you to fall in love with me.

But you can't.

At least not yet.

Forgetting What Love Feels Like

*Lately I've come to terms with being completely
alone but I'm not sure I will ever be at peace with it*

*The empty feeling of not being able to share my love
with another aches the tender part of my heart*

Regardless, I'm filled with love

*It seeps through my skin and runs out
of my mouth in every "hello" and "good
morning" and "how are you?"*

*Small talk and waving to strangers wouldn't
compare to coming home into someone's arms.*

*It's been so long since I've been able to stare
at the universe through someone's eyes*

*I hope I won't spend the rest of my life
searching for a hand to hold.*

Voices

The wind carries your voice to my ear

Almost as gently as the sound of the distant waves
falling towards the Mediterranean shoreline

It's beautiful in a way, how the strong
breeze plays tricks on us

The ocean answers when people don't

A Game Without A Winner

Loving you is like chasing my shadow

       It's inevitable that I will never catch you

No matter how hard I try or what effort I give

       You will never truly love me back

Fall Apart

Our love still stands

But it won't last

We are not an ancient ruin

Building a love that we never fixed

Gives us the chance to fall apart

Downstream

I'm sorry if everything seems so sudden and what I say will drive you away from this extraordinary connection that pulls the two of us together like magnets but I've had the need to get something off of my chest

I'm not sure that's the proper way to put it but I've been biting my tongue too much and hitting the backspace button more often than not

It's hard for me to say what I mean because we have these standards to live up to

That have been engraved in our souls of how we should act and how to correctly form words into sentences

The list could go on for eternity but I just want to tell you what I've kept restricted from saying out loud

There are an infinite amount of thoughts I haven't put into conversation

But I've decided to unleash it into words that in the least bit could not even begin to describe everything I want to say

I'm certain that the word "love" has been overused so I've been refraining from using it

But in this world we live in it seems to be the only thing keeping everyone's hopes up

This world needs a great deal of amends to make it beautiful again, I'm well aware

Ever since the day you've entered my life, my entire world has been lit up from every dark street corner in the edges of my mind

Things have been so much brighter from the planet placed in my head

It's cliché to say one person can change the world

Because there are seven billion people on this earth and multiple species of plants and animals

We still have a whole universe to discover

I've learned a number of times that chances are usually only given once

I really don't want to let this one disappear

As I've said before, whatever is going on between us is why I'm trying so hard not to let it go away with the acceptable way to profess feelings.

I'm not going to let these words wash away down the fork in the river of what we call life.

*Rivers seem endless but this could be the
mouth of the river and our last likelihood
of ever getting to say what we mean.*

*There are thousands of languages and
dialects that are spoken in the present day
but none of them could have the words
to describe my feelings for you*

*I'm tired of letting everything slip away
because the hesitation and feeling in my
stomach of saying the wrong things.*

There will never be a perfect time for anything.

So I think the moment is now.

Homeless Heart

I followed my heart to many places

I left a part of myself in that city

Home is where the heart is

Art Is Not Meant To Be Beautiful

She's a disregarded work of art

A few brush strokes shy from being a pastel painting hung up inside of one of those fancy galleries or on the blank wall space in the dining room next to the china cabinet.

She's the photographs of the rivers and streams five miles out of town that are framed in the local coffee shop that's running out of business

Her voice is the classical symphonies played on damaged cassette tapes, and the sound of wind whistling through the brittle orange trees in the autumn air

She's a little less chiseled than the sculpture behind the window in the new shop off of 4th street

She's black and grey, the color of the clouds before a thunderstorm

She's anything and everything

And I am her artist

Forget About Love

One day I'll forget the sound of your voice and the color of your dreamy eyes

My morning coffee will no longer taste of your lips

Your side of the bed won't smell like you anymore

I can walk passed our favorite restaurant without it reminding me of you

I could finally look into the glimmer of the night sky and not wish on every shooting star for you

One day I'll forget about you and everything won't conjure up a memory

But right now that's all I'm left with.

Bridge

We were two separate souls

Living life far apart

Fate led me towards you

And you to me

Eventually our love crumbled

And we broke away from each other

I'm still in one piece

I hope you are too

But it's not worth it to build a bridge between us

Our love is not strong enough

From the Grape Vine

Grape   *too*

　　vines　　　　　*travelers*

　　　　are

They can grow to visit further places

And their leaves can fly away with the wind

All while being rooted to the ground

Heart of the City

Your fear of leaving home will fade away as you learn to find comfort in crowded subways and unfamiliar faces. You'll realize that the streets are your canvas and your feet is the paint. Being on the edge of tall buildings will no longer scare you. Eating alone will become a routine, even though it was something that you've never liked to do before. You'll put layers of blankets on you when you're cold at night with no one asleep next to you to keep you warm. Five flights of stairs isn't too much anymore, but you'd still wish your apartment building would have an elevator. Greeting cards from relatives that come in the mail mean so much more to you now that you've been on your own for so long. Maybe it hasn't been awhile, but your small town heart is turning into the kind of a city-goer.

I Bet My Heart on You

Back in June I went to a woman who read my palm to tell me what the future holds for me. She told me that I would fall in love this September. At the time, people told me that the fortune teller swindled me. They told me I cheated God's plan in finding out my future.

I woke up on September 1st in a hostel to expect nothing less than to discover the beautiful city of Barcelona. But then I met you.

I don't regret any of our adventures. No, nothing beats horchata and churros at La Rambla and getting lost in the gothic quarter. I reminisce the time we watched the sunset at the beach.

Maybe the fortune teller forgot to say that if I were to fall in love with a traveler like you, we would wash away in the Mediterranean Sea along with our footprints in the sand.

I wish I would've taken more pictures of you like the monuments we saw. But I'm not so sure.

Maybe losing you after your flight to Morocco was God's punishment for me. It's been a month since I've been home and I still haven't felt any butterflies in my stomach.

I think I cheated fate.

More Time

If I could be everywhere at once

I would stay behind in the places I've traveled

Without the worry of ending my journey

The clock keeps ticking

And I wish I could stop time

When I leave the bells will ring

A new hour will begin

Lost

I see the world in your eyes

I could get endlessly lost in them

If I drift away in the wrong direction

I don't know if I'll find my way back

Wish

You were my every wish

That I thought would be granted

But we woke up from our dream

And the universe pulled you away

I thought your love was promised to me

You and I never came true

Forever and More

I could wait forever

For you to come back

Maybe it's the color of your eyes

Or the sound of your voice

That has kept me captivated

Since the day I've met you

Life guided us in different directions

I hope we'll cross paths again one day

Things that Fall

The ocean's waves rise and fall

That's not the only one of all

The stars so little and bright

Come shooting down through the night

The raindrops that seem to fly

Tumble from the gloomy sky

The orange leaves crumbling pieces

Soar from its branches during the autumn season

Of all the things that have to fall

Me for you is the hardest of them all

Barcelona Charm

I've sat back for years watching people fall in love in my hometown thinking I'd never get a chance at it.

Being midway across the world, I've only expected to fall in love with the places I've seen. I'd never thought the stranger sitting four seats down from me at the internet cafe would be such an important part of my journey.

I'd like to thank you for our memories.

Walks down La Rambla and our spontaneous dance together in Plaça Catalunya makes up for every single prom or homecoming I was never asked to.

I know you wouldn't know the importance of prom in America, because you're from Argentina. I can assure you I'd rather aimlessly wander the streets of Barcelona with you at 1AM than attend a high school dance ever again.

The Mediterranean Sea could probably fit into your eyes. But only at sunset when the water looks murky underneath the bright colors of the sky. Because when we sat on the rocks at the Barceloneta, I saw the endless ocean reflect on them when you looked my way.

Thank you for all of the drunken kisses and for trying to squeeze in my bunk just to sleep next to me. Even though we're out of school, you've gave me the feeling of young love that I've always missed out on.

Maybe Barcelona should be called the city of love. I've fallen in love with this place, and you've made me love it even more.

Traveling comes a price. You left for Morocco this morning, just like I'm leaving to go home to California in 2 weeks. We've spent 5 days together for what seems like so much longer. It was unforgettable, you are unforgettable.

Once I board my plane back to France, I will leave whatever we had in this city. I don't love you, but you've filled in the gap of what I've dreamed of feeling for a long time. I wish you a safe trip to Casa Blanca, and wherever you plan on travelling after that.

Our hearts wander just like we do. It's the price you have to pay being a traveler. But eventually mine wants to go home.

Waves

My dreams are embedded in the sand

I am the waves that collide with the shoreline

Washing into the land

I will float away eventually

To find another dream

Next Stop

You are hard to understand like the subway map

I'm going to have to go through every tunnel

To figure you out

I don't know where you are

But I'm heading towards the next stop

And I'm not going to look for you there

Heaven

Maybe we've all seen a bit of heaven

*There is unworldly beauty that can
be seen by the human eye*

If heaven still awaits

*It will strike us more than the
glimpses we've witnessed*

Trees

Trees live a lonely life

They can see the world from way up high

But have to stay planted to the ground

Take Time to Smell the Roses

If the world was a rose

It would take me an eternity to inhale its scent

I am still climbing up its thorns

To see the beauty it holds

The Sun Shine and the Earth

I am jealous of the sun

It is able to shine down on this earth

And explore all of its beauty

The sun has seen the world

More than anyone ever could

Here and There

*There are masterpieces in places
you wouldn't expect*

*You can find magnificence in
every part of the world*

Wandering is not measured in distance

You just have to open your eyes

We are all traveling souls

We are all on a journey

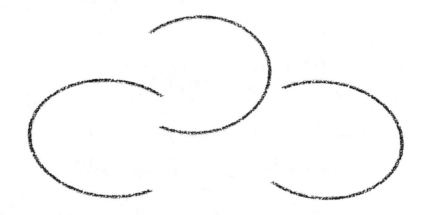

threestatesofmind.tumblr.com

Author Biography

Anna Quimpo Maguire is a Filipino-American writer.

She runs an aesthetic-themed blog that features
her poetry under the name Three States of Mind.
Her love for writing began at age twelve when
she attended a local poetry workshop.

To this day, she is an avid traveler at her own expense
while being a college student as well. As a liberal studies
major, she plans on teaching upon obtaining her degree.

Maguire is the founder of the Quimpo-Maguire
Foundation, a charity that grants scholarships to students
at a Philippine public high school located in Quezon City.

Anna Quimpo Maguire currently resides up
in the mountains of California, remaining
to live a life full of adventure.

Printed in the United States
By Bookmasters